To Keith and Dennise for supporting my journey
as a squirrel in a sky full of stars —K.E.

For my high school drama teacher, Mr. Bob Hotze —J.E.

Text copyright © 2020 by Kamen Edwards
Jacket art and interior illustrations copyright © 2020 by Jeffrey Ebbeler

All rights reserved. Published in the United States by Doubleday, an imprint of
Random House Children's Books, a division of Penguin Random House LLC, New York.

Doubleday and the colophon are registered trademarks of Penguin Random House LLC.

Visit us on the Web! rhcbooks.com

Educators and librarians, for a variety of teaching tools, visit us at
RHTeachersLibrarians.com

Library of Congress Cataloging-in-Publication Data
Names: Edwards, Kamen, author. | Ebbeler, Jeffrey, illustrator.
Title: The one and only Dylan St. Claire / by Kamen Edwards ;
illustrated by Jeffrey Ebbeler.
Description: New York : Doubleday Books for Young Readers, 2020. | Audience: Ages 4–8.
Summary: "Dylan St. Claire faces a week of anguish when he fails to get cast as the star
in the school musical and lands the role of a squirrel instead." —Provided by publisher.
Identifiers: LCCN 2019028509 (print) | LCCN 2019028510 (ebook)
ISBN 978 1 9848 9346 8 (hardcover) | ISBN 978-1-9848-9347-5 (library binding) |
ISBN 978-1-9848-9348-2 (ebook)
Subjects: CYAC: Theater—Fiction. | Acting—Fiction.
Classification: LCC PZ7.1.E294 On 2020 (print) | LCC PZ7.1.E294 (ebook) |
DDC [E]—dc23

Interior design by Nicole Gastonguay

MANUFACTURED IN CHINA
10 9 8 7 6 5 4 3 2 1

First Edition

THE 'ONE AND ONLY
DYLAN ST. CLAIRE

By **Kamen Edwards**

Illustrated by **Jeffrey Ebbeler**

Doubleday Books
for Young Readers

Every morning when the sun comes up, the stars disappear. Well, all but one: Dylan St. Claire. And today is the day he plans on shining the brightest.

It's audition day for our school musical! This year it's all about the solar system . . . and I just know I'm going to be a star! Literally, I'm going to play The Star! A role I was BORN for.
Dylan
Dylan

Dylan spent all summer perfecting "his craft" at Mama Rose's Day Camp for Li'l Superstars, where he worked on his . . .

Jazz

Tap

Vocal training

Mime

All his hard work has come down to this! It's time for Dylan to shuffle-ball-change off to school and earn his spot in outer space!

But here's the thing about seeing a star shining during the daytime. A lot of people don't know what to make of it.

If Mama Rose's Day Camp
for Li'l Superstars had a class
on how to make an entrance,
Dylan could teach it!

Should we tell him there aren't any auditions?
Don't ruin his day. He's wearing tap shoes.

It turns out Dylan may have misunderstood how this was all going to work. . . .

Okay, class. It's time for me to tell you what role you'll be playing in our musical! Our sun will be . . . Becky! Our star will be . . . Kirsten!

Like any good actor, Dylan is very in touch with his emotions. At Mama Rose's Day Camp for Li'l Superstars, he learned a breathing exercise to use when his emotions get the best of him. . . .

AHHHHH!
What am I going to do?! The entire school year is ruined! My LIFE is ruined!!! My acting career is OVER before it even BEGAN!

What should have been Dylan's favorite week of the year is quickly turning into his worst nightmare.

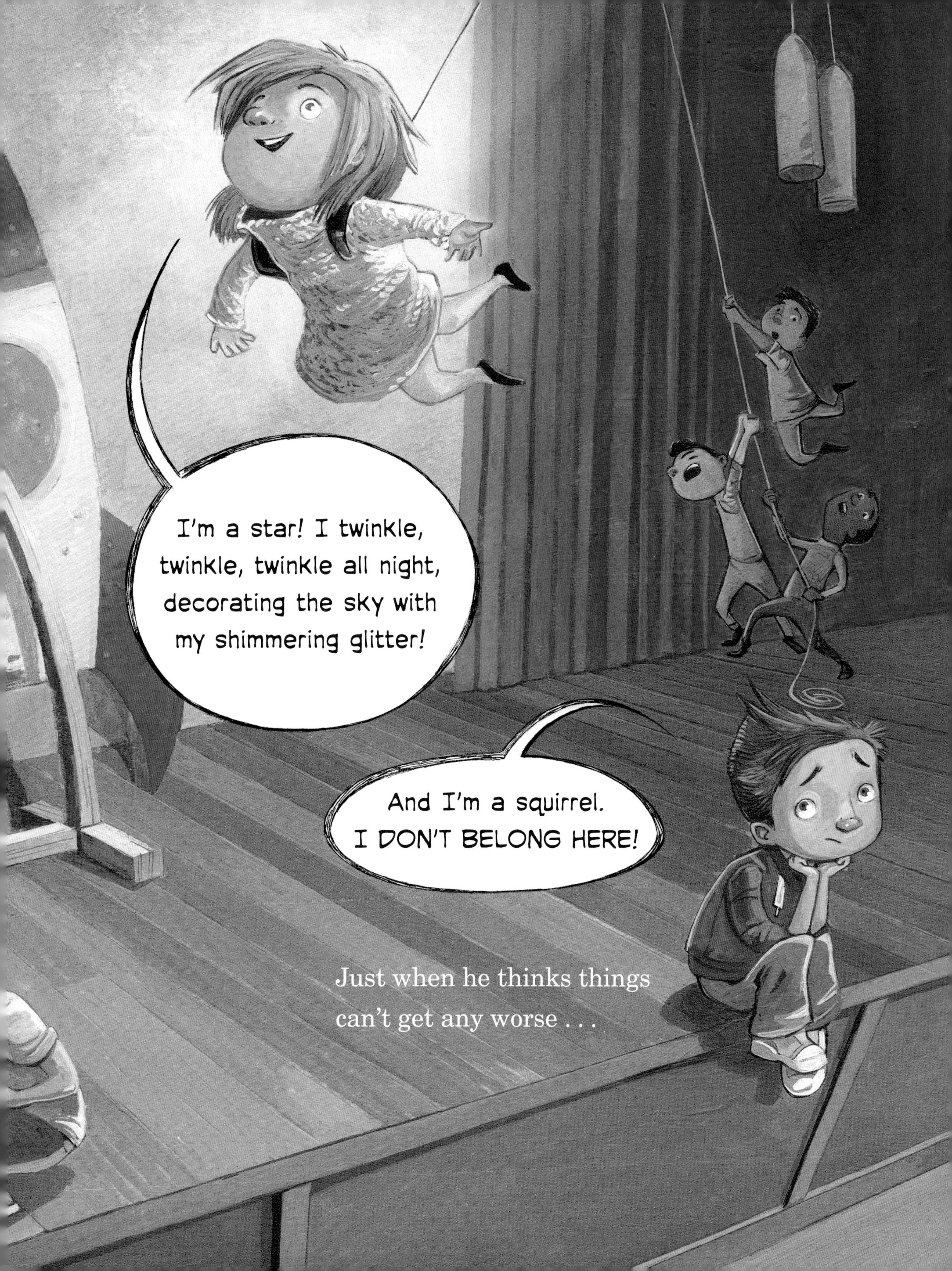

Just when he thinks things can't get any worse . . .

Apparently, Dylan isn't the only one having a hard week.

That's easy for you to say. You love the spotlight. Plus, the squirrel is the best part of the show!
Hmmm . . . I guess there IS a certain whimsical spirit to the character. The ONLY squirrel EVER to go to space! By the rings of Saturn, you're right! It's my duty as an actor and friend to squirrels to boldly go where no squirrel has ever gone before!

And just like that, Dylan begins his quest to be the best squirrel his school has ever seen—nay, the WORLD has ever seen!

Dylan may not have been cast as
the star, but he has certainly found
his own way to shine like one.

Look out,
universe . . . this
squirrel is ready for
blastoff!

And that's why I, the first squirrel-stronaut in outer space, am absolutely NUTS for the solar system!

There are millions of stars in the sky, and from the earth they all look the same. Each twinkles and shines just like the ones next to it.

But not Dylan St. Claire. In a sky full of stars . . .

he's a squirrel.